Sticker Dolly Dressing
Best Friends

Illustrated by Jo Moore
Designed by Vicky Barker
Written by Lucy Bowman

Contents

2   Meet the dolls
4   Picnic time
6   Movie night
8   Karaoke
10 Dressing up
12 Birthday cake
13 Surprise party
14 A day at the beach
16 Horse riding
18 Ice cream
20 Dance studio
22 Sleepover
24 My best friend
    Stickers

The back cover folds out so you can "park"
spare stickers there while you dress the dolls.

Meet the dolls

Amber, Lacy and Sophia are three best friends. They love spending time together and are always there for each other. Today they're in Lacy's treehouse, relaxing and reading magazines.

Amber is very creative. She is always making things to give to her friends, like beaded bracelets and hand-painted T-shirts.

Sophia loves to read books and write stories. She likes following the latest fashions in magazines, as well as creating her own new look.

Lacy loves the outdoors. She thinks up fun activities to do with her friends. She has a dog, named Puggles, who follows her everywhere.

Picnic time

The sun is shining, so the dolls are visiting their local park for a picnic. They've brought lots of delicious food to eat, including chocolate chip cookies made by Amber. Lacy wants to play an energetic game of frisbee before they eat.

Movie night

The dolls have gone to see a movie – last week it was action, tonight, they're watching a comedy with a funny actress in it. Amber has bought a large box of popcorn for them all to share.

Karaoke

The dolls all love music and are singing along to a karaoke game. Lacy likes to make up dance moves to go with the songs, while Sophia focuses on her singing to try to get a higher score.

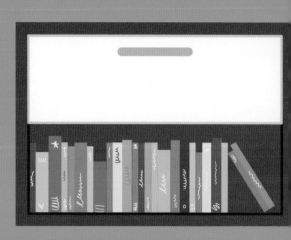

Dressing up

Amber, Lacy and Sophia are in the changing room of a fancy department store. They've been shopping all day trying to find the perfect dresses and accessories to match. There are so many gorgeous things to choose from.

1 2 3

Birthday cake

Amber has baked a lemon sponge cake for Lacy's birthday. She is decorating it with ribbon and flowers made from white and yellow icing.

Surprise party

Sophia is preparing a room for Lacy's birthday party. She has hung up bright balloons and streamers, and gathered the birthday gifts together ready for Lacy to unwrap. Now she's just waiting for Lacy to come in so that she can shout 'Surprise!'.

A day at the beach

The dolls are having fun on a sunny beach. Amber and Sophia have brought their boogie boards with them to ride the waves, while Lacy and Puggles are going to look for crabs.

Horse riding

Sophia, Lacy and Amber are all good at riding. Lacy is looking forward to learning to jump, while Sophia and Amber want to learn dressage (where the horse does special steps in a rhythm). They've brought carrots to feed to their horses as treats.

Ice cream

The dolls are buying ice creams. There are so many different kinds to choose from, everything from gooey banana splits to hot fudge sundaes. Sophia has ordered a sundae of her own creation – vanilla ice cream and fresh strawberries, topped with nuts, marshmallows and chocolate sauce. Delicious!

Dance studio

The dolls are at a dance rehearsal, as they are soon going to be performing a routine live on stage. They turn the music up while they dance, and wear loose clothes and sneakers that they can move around in easily.

Sleepover

The dolls are having so much fun at a sleepover at Amber's house. They've made their own pizzas with yummy toppings and listened to the latest pop songs. Now it's time for bed, they'll get in their sleeping bags and tell each other spooky stories!

My best friend

Here you can create a picture of
your best friend. Fill in the eyes,
hair and face so it looks like your
friend, then add accessories
from the sticker page.

First published in 2016 by Usborne Publishing Limited, 83-85 Saffron Hill, London EC1N 8RT, United Kingdom. usborne.com
Copyright © 2016 Usborne Publishing Limited. The name Usborne and the Balloon logo are registered trade marks of Usborne Publishing Limited.
All rights reserved. No part of this publication may be reproduced, stored in a retrieval system or transmitted in any form or by any means
without prior permission of the publisher. First published in America 2016. This edition published 2023. UE.

Birthday cake page 12

Surprise party page 13

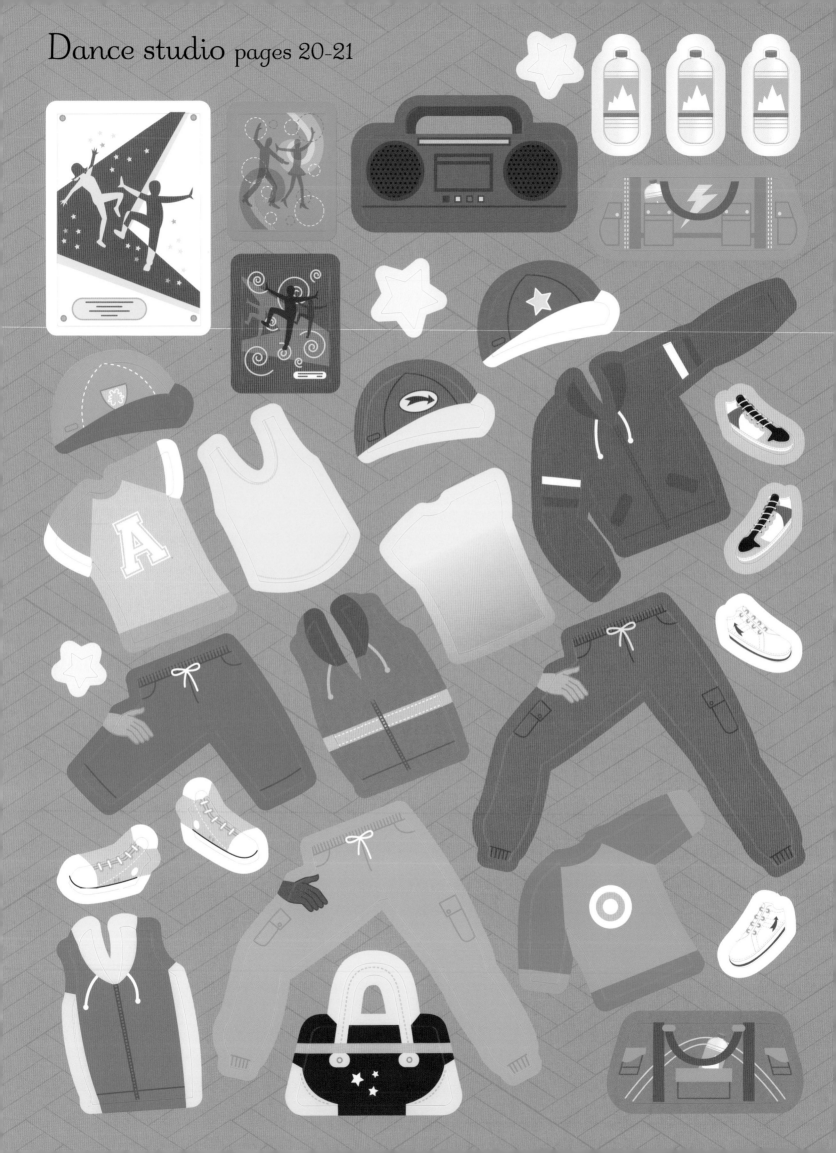

Sleepover pages 22-23

My best friend page 24

Write your best friend's name here.